Peculiar Produce

The Alphabet Coloring Book

By Moya & Grau

HAND PRESS INK

Peculiar Produce - The Alphabet Coloring Book
© 2021 Moya & Grau, Hand Press Ink

ISBN: 978-1-7371085-4-2

Typeset in grau-hand-3

PeculiarProduce.org
HandPressInk.com

About Peculiar Produce

Peculiar Produce presents opportunities to learn about uncommon foods and discover the names of children from different cultures. With its alliterative text and aspirational vocabulary, the book encourages discussion around the variety in fruits and vegetables while accentuating their differences and imperfections.

Exploring the characters, their shapes, and their actions will open conversations around using affirming words, uplifting actions towards others, body inclusivity, and encouraging healthy eating.

We hope you enjoy this interactive coloring book as much as we do! Thank you.

Dedicated to
the artists and creators
in everyone.

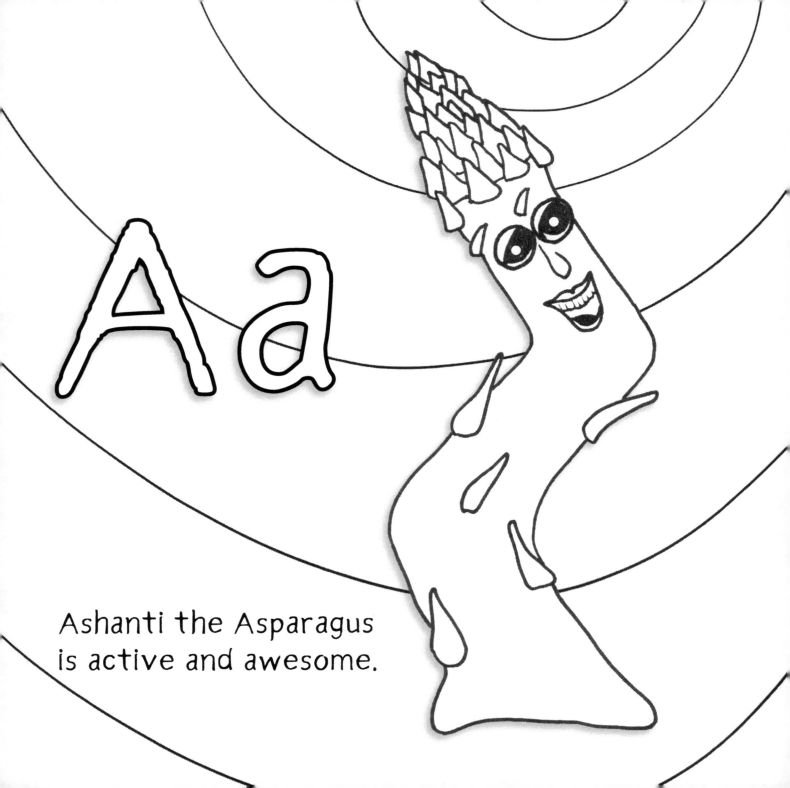

Aa

Ashanti the Asparagus
is active and awesome.

Blake the Beet
is bold and brave.

Casey the Carrot
is cute and crunchy.

Cc

Dd

Dylan the Durian
is different and delicious.

Durian (dur-ee-uhn)

Emery the Eggplant
is energetic and excellent.

Ee

F f

Fabio the Fennel has
fabulous frizzyfronds.

Gabe the Garlic
gives goofy gazes.

Hh

Hudson the Honeydew
is heavy and happy.

Izumi the Ice Cream Bean
is interesting and important.

Jaden the Jicama
is jolly and joyous.

Jicama (HEE-kuh-muh)

K K

Kai the Kale
is keen to be kind.

L l

Logan the Lychee
is light and lovely.

Lychee (lee-chee)

Mm

Milo the Mushroom
is majestic in the
moonlight.

Nash the Nectarine
is notably nourishing.

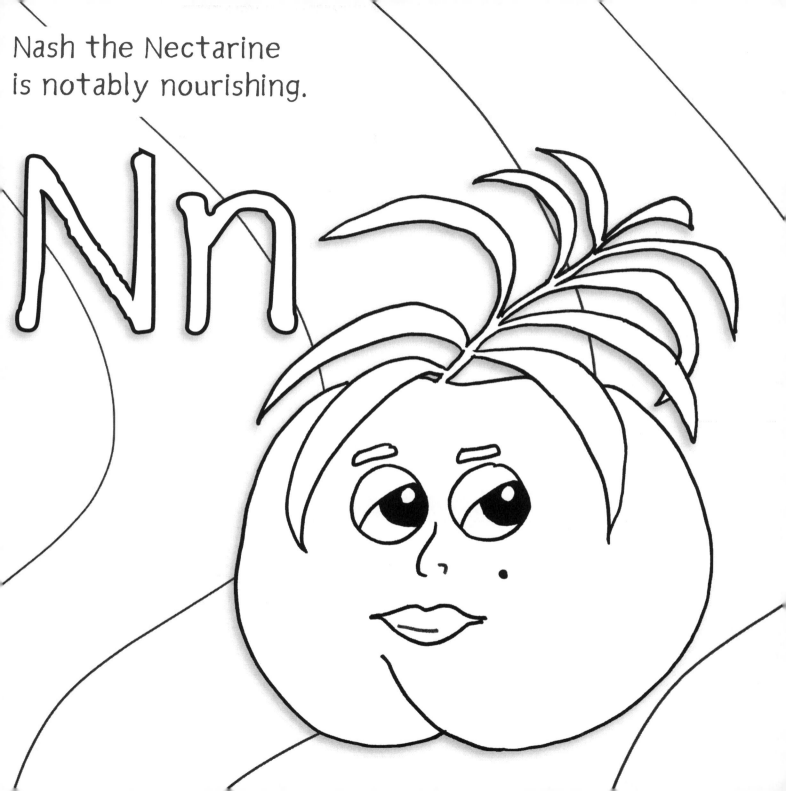

Oakley the Okra
is outstanding and original.

Peyton the Pineapple
is prickly and proud.

Qq

Quinn the Quince
is quaint and quiet.

Quince (kwints)

Ridley the Radish
is robust and radiant.

Rr

Sydney the Strawberry
is smart and sweet.

Tolu the Tomato
is tasty and terrific.

Udo the Hawaiian
Ulu has unusual uses.

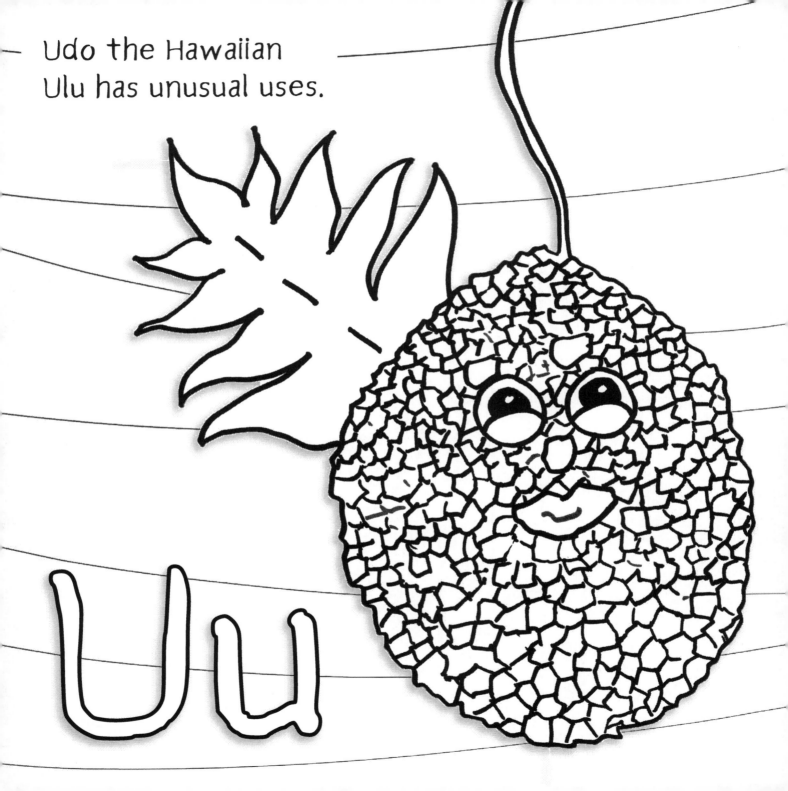

Uu

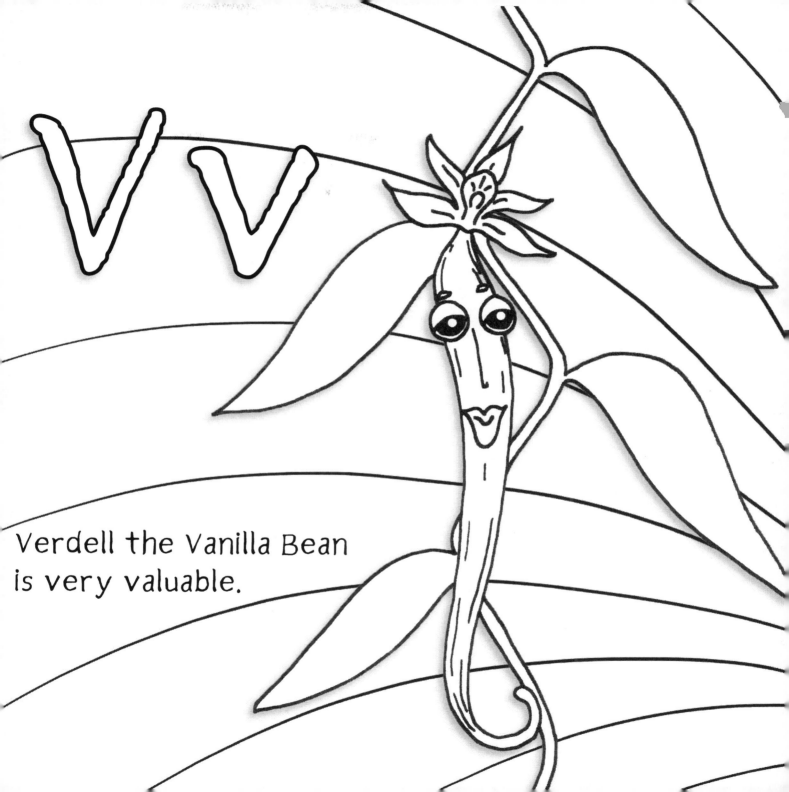

Verdell the Vanilla Bean
is very valuable.

Ww

Wakapa
the Water Chestnut
is wet and wild.

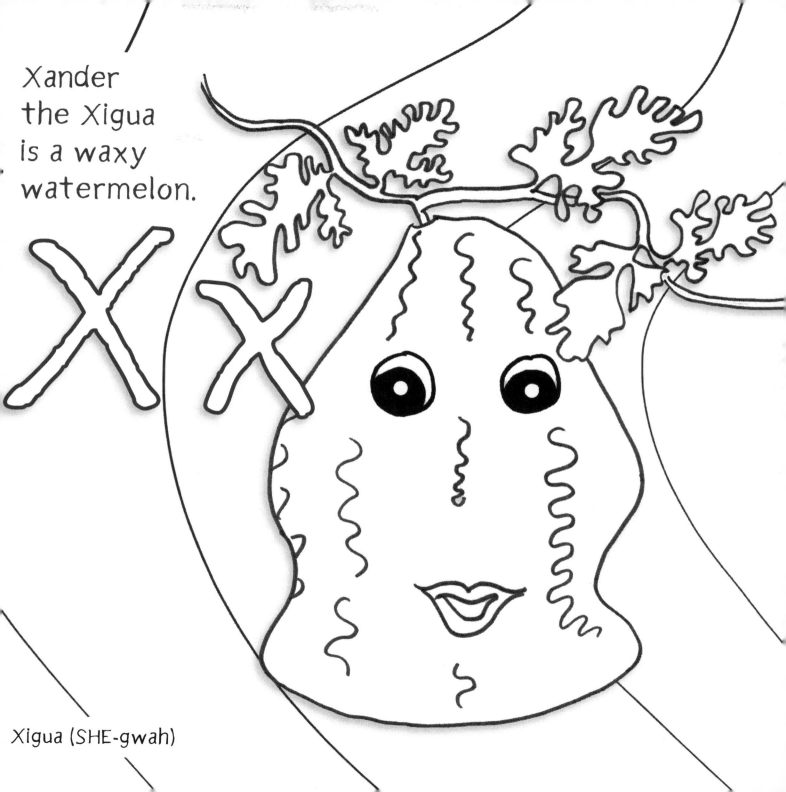

Xander
the Xigua
is a waxy
watermelon.

Xigua (SHE-gwah)

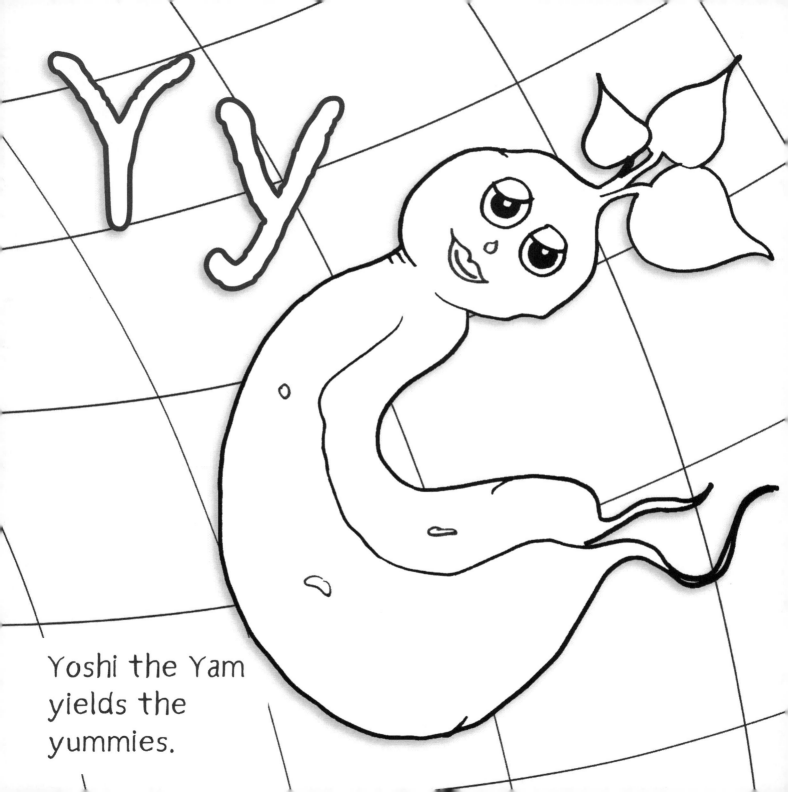

Yoshi the Yam
yields the
yummies.

Zola the Zucchini
is zippy and zany.

Happy growing, cooking, and eating!

Peculiar Produce fun facts!

Asparagus takes three years to grow! If asparagus is covered in dirt while it grows, it comes out white and not green.

Beets can be eaten from top to toe! Beets are edible from the top of the greens to the bottom of the roots.

Carrots are usually orange in color but purple, red, white, and yellow varieties also exist.

Durian can grow to be twelve inches high and up to seven pounds!

Eggplant is called Aubergine in the United Kingdom and Brinjal in some parts of Asia.

Fennel tastes sweet like licorice and can grow up to eight feet tall!

Garlic is great for people but can get some pets sick!

Honeydew has nicknames like the 'melon tuna' in parts of Latin America and the 'Bailan melon' in China.

An Ice Cream Bean comes from South America, is used for medicine, and has tasty pods that are used in desserts!

Jicama can be peeled like a potato and eaten raw. Raw jicama is very similar to raw apples - light, crisp, and sweet.

Kale is a superfood, with many different varieties. It's a very strong plant and can even survive freezing temperatures.

Lychees have a sweet taste and can be made into sauces and jams. Lychee seeds are poisonous and should not be eaten.

Mushrooms have their own immune systems.

Nectarines take their name from 'nectar' - the food of the gods.

The Okra plant can be used to make flour, paper, and ropes! It also grows beautiful flowers.

The top of a Pineapple, after cleaning and drying, can be planted in soil and a new plant will grow.

Quince are mainly used to make jelly since the raw fruit is too hard to eat.

Radishes are easy and fast to grow, even kids can do it!

Strawberries are the only fruit that have their seeds on the outside of their skin.

Tomatoes are a fruit! The word tomato comes from the Indigenous American Nahuatl language word 'tomatl'.

Ulu is also known as 'breadfruit' and can be mashed, fried, stewed, or even made into custard.

Vanilla is difficult to grow. It is the only orchid known to produce an edible fruit and is one of the most expensive spices in the world.

Water Chestnuts are light, crunchy, and very nutritious. They are not nuts at all but instead, the aquatic tuber of a grass native to Asia.

Xigua is pronounced 'she-gwah' and is the Chinese word for watermelon. Containers can be used to grow xigua into unusual shapes.

Yams are inexpensive, easy to grow and come in many colors. More than 200 kinds of yams are grown around the world.

The flowers of a Zucchini plant are also edible and delicious!

Made in the USA
Middletown, DE
01 March 2023